ISBN: 978-1-7781095-0-8
First printing, 2022

Illustrated by: Arash Jahani

Dedication

This book is dedicated to my son Warren for
his huge support and guidance in this venture

In this pocket you will find
A teensy, tiny tooth of mine.
So while I sleep where dreams are made,
Let's see if you can make a trade.
~Author unknown

Lenny and the Tooth Town Team is Oriane Falkenstein's first book. Young children will hope the characters appear in follow-up adventures. In the story, the tiny fairies encounter obstacles that seem insurmountable. With ingenuity and teamwork, they succeed despite the challenges. Young readers (and listeners) will absorb the "can do" message and enjoy the evocative illustrations, gasping in the tense moments. Lenny, a Tooth Town hero, scored some of the heavy wisdom teeth for building materials in Tooth Town. Falkenstein imparts more than one valuable message to young readers. It is okay to dream big and pursue challenges some may think impossible. Lenny's team makes it possible. They fly on a special trip to a dentist's office in the tooth taxi. Then math and comparisons become part of the story with the weight of a feather and a wisdom tooth. What do dentists do with pulled teeth anyway? Now we have the answer!

Boys and girls alike will enjoy the story. The illustrations alone offer delight to both adults and children, with amazing vibrant images on every page. Children ages 6-8 will enjoy the book on their own and younger children will ask for it at bedtime, especially when they lose their baby teeth.

My favorite parts are the tense moments when the power blips out trapping Lenny inside with his team outside and how after he almost passes out, he tells himself to *find a way*. I also admire Lenny's drive to succeed for a bigger reason beyond increasing his own status. He is thinking about how the wisdom teeth are needed for a higher purpose – to build a spa for tired tooth team members.

Parents and teachers, there are more messages and valuable teachings packed in this book. I leave you to discover some of them on your own.

Rusti L Lehay
Collaborative / Immersion Editor
www.rustilehay.info

"Let's go!" shouted Lenny and in a scurry of activity and a blur of movement they were off...down...down...down in the shimmering moonlight on their special quest.

Outside as the stars glimmered, the little boy smiled in his sleep, his thoughts far away. Under his pillow was tucked his first big TOOTH.

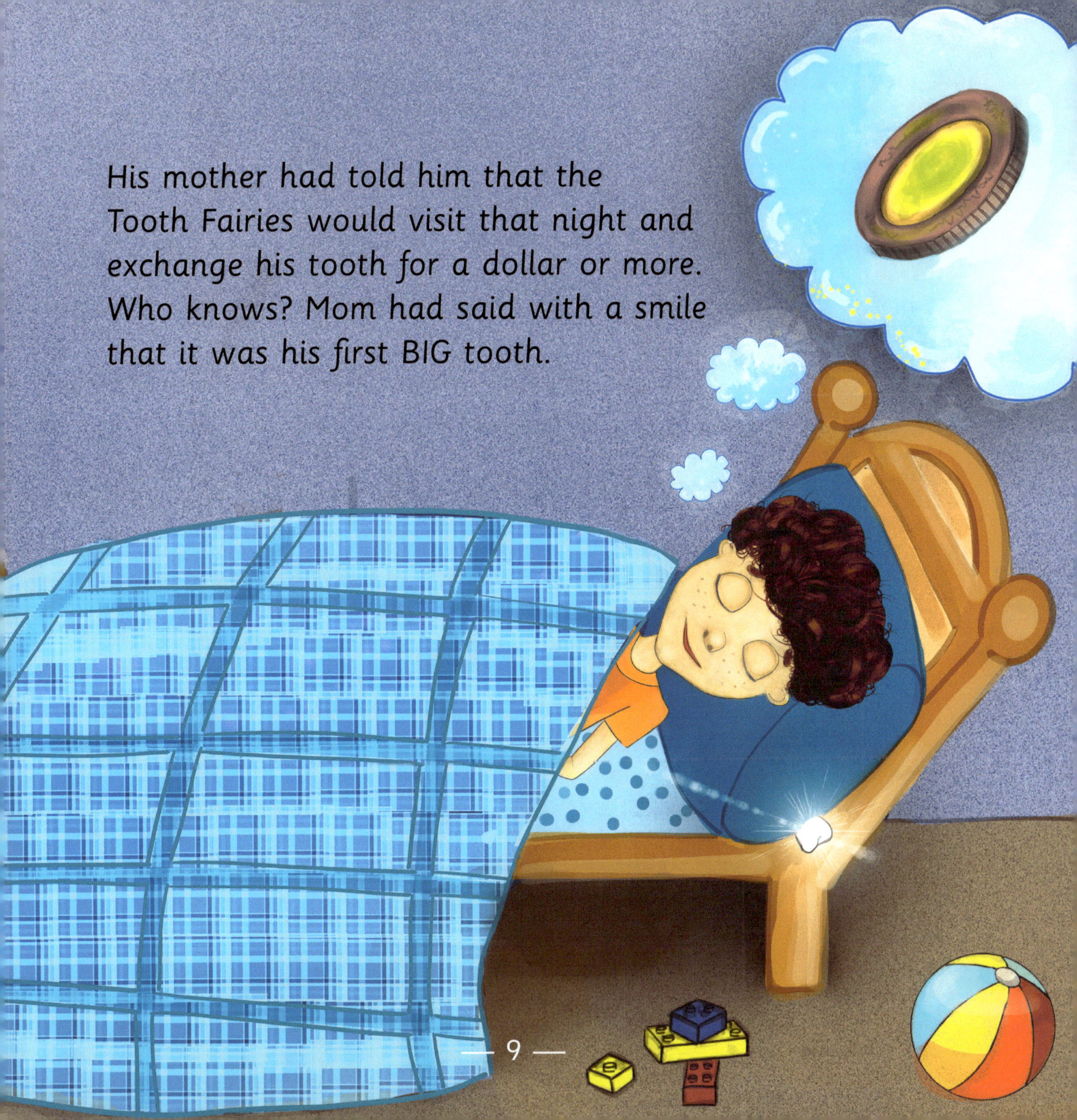

His mother had told him that the Tooth Fairies would visit that night and exchange his tooth for a dollar or more. Who knows? Mom had said with a smile that it was his first BIG tooth.

The Tooth Fairies gathered around the house, whispering and scurrying. Lenny gave instructions to the Tooth Fairy Driver to wait right outside the window. He grabbed the Tooth Tote.

Excited, the fairies rushed in. Tooth Fairies are
very small and very light – as light as a feather.

As the boy slept, Lenny reached under the pillow
and squeezed and wiggled himself in.
He began to tug at the envelope
that held the TOOTH. It was
hard work! The Tooth Fairies
held on to Lenny's tiny legs
so that he could stretch
and stretch and...

finally he managed to pull out the corner of the envelope. The fairies squealed with delight as they all peeked inside... another TOOTH and ohhhh such a BIG one!

Lenny reached into his pouch, drew out his special Tooth Wand and flipped it in the air. When he woke, the boy would be thrilled to find shiny coins under his pillow, just as he had dreamed about that night!

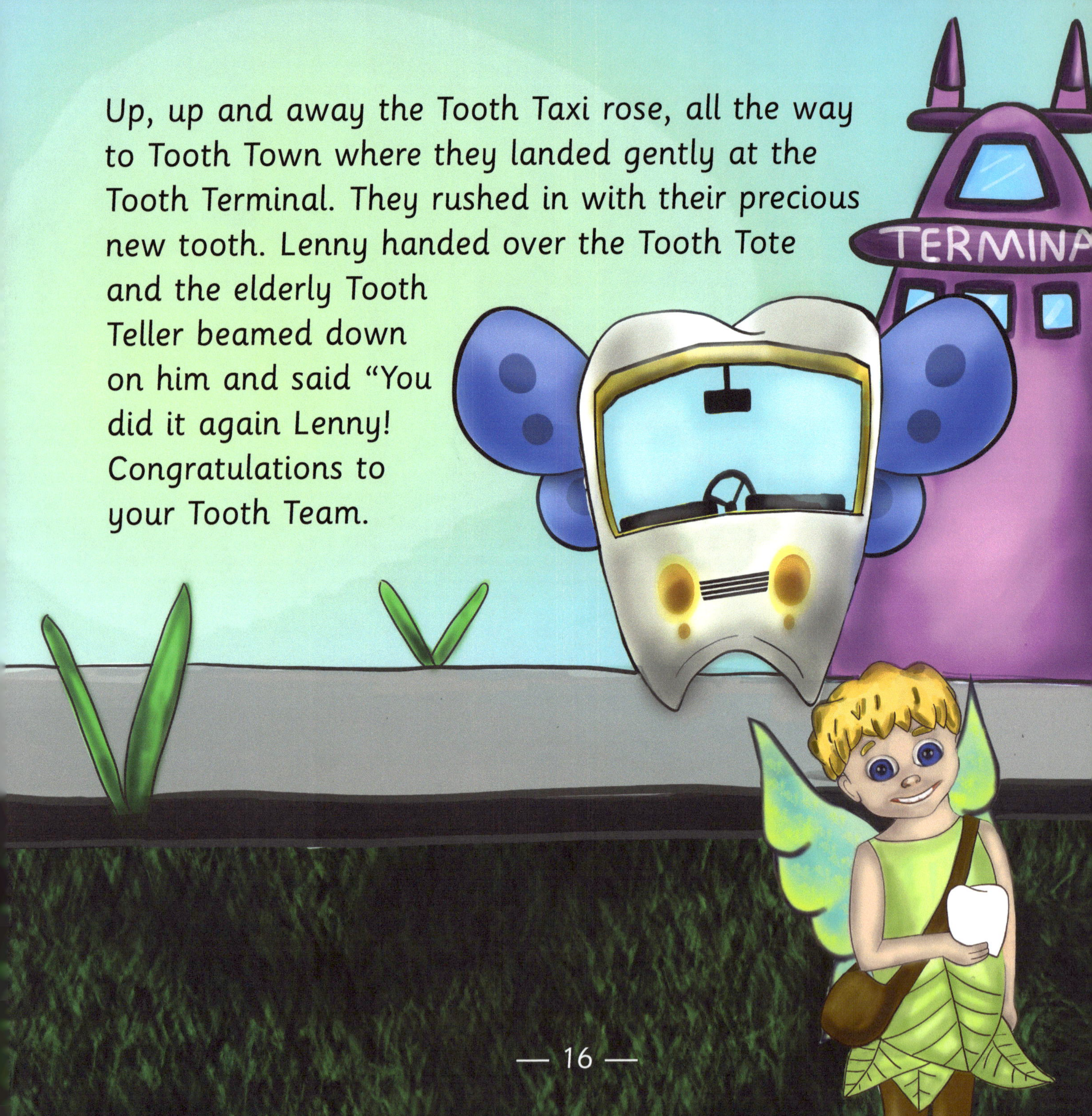

Up, up and away the Tooth Taxi rose, all the way to Tooth Town where they landed gently at the Tooth Terminal. They rushed in with their precious new tooth. Lenny handed over the Tooth Tote and the elderly Tooth Teller beamed down on him and said "You did it again Lenny! Congratulations to your Tooth Team.

TT

TOOTH TERMINAL TUCK SHOP

Lenny and the other fairies smiled as they left the Tooth Teller. It was time to stop by the Tooth Terminal Tuck Shop and share stories with the other Tooth Teams. Lenny looked around at Tooth Town.

It had grown and grown and he could spot new developments popping up, all built of shiny new TEETH. His favourite was the Tooth House where the little tables and chairs were all built of baby teeth and where the baby fairies were taken care of during the day.

Down the road was Tooth Town's only school. It had grown over the years as the Tooth Fairy population increased. It was a solid structure and Lenny was so proud that he had contributed many of the Wisdom Teeth that held up the walls. WISDOM TEETH were every Tooth Team Fairy's dream catch!

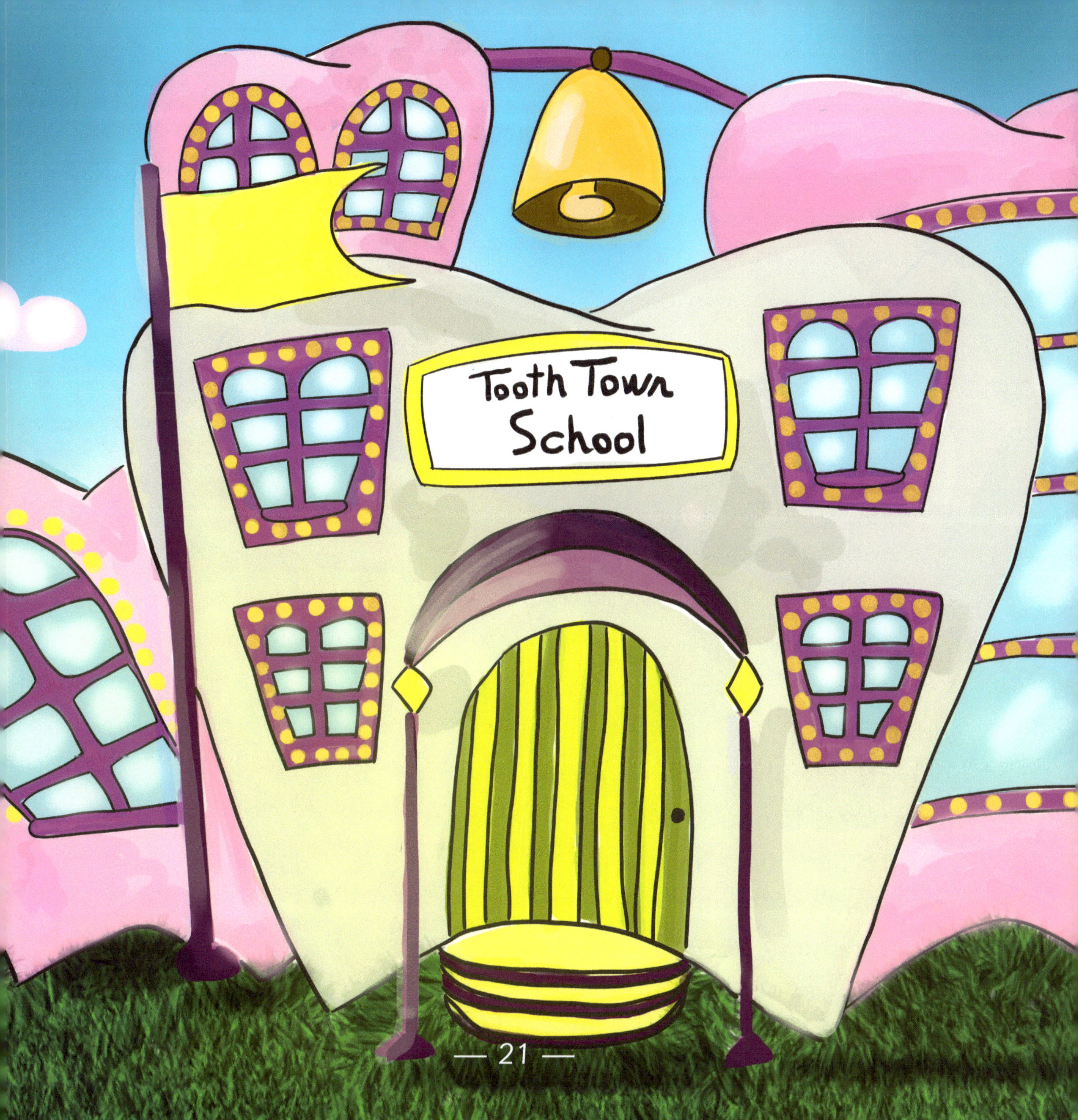
Tooth Town
School

Lenny and
the other
Tooth Fairy
leaders loved to
swap stories about some of their
adventures. Lenny knew that everyone
loved to hear his story of
Dr. Cuspid's Wisdom Teeth over
and over again, especially the
new Tooth Fairies on the team.

They all personally hoped that they would be able to do what Lenny had managed to do that long difficult night, when there was a MAGIC POWER OUTAGE, and Lenny had been trapped all alone in Dr Cuspid's office.

Lenny always told the story with pride and he never let on that he had felt so frightened that night. Deep down, he knew that he had had a lucky break and he always felt grateful for that.

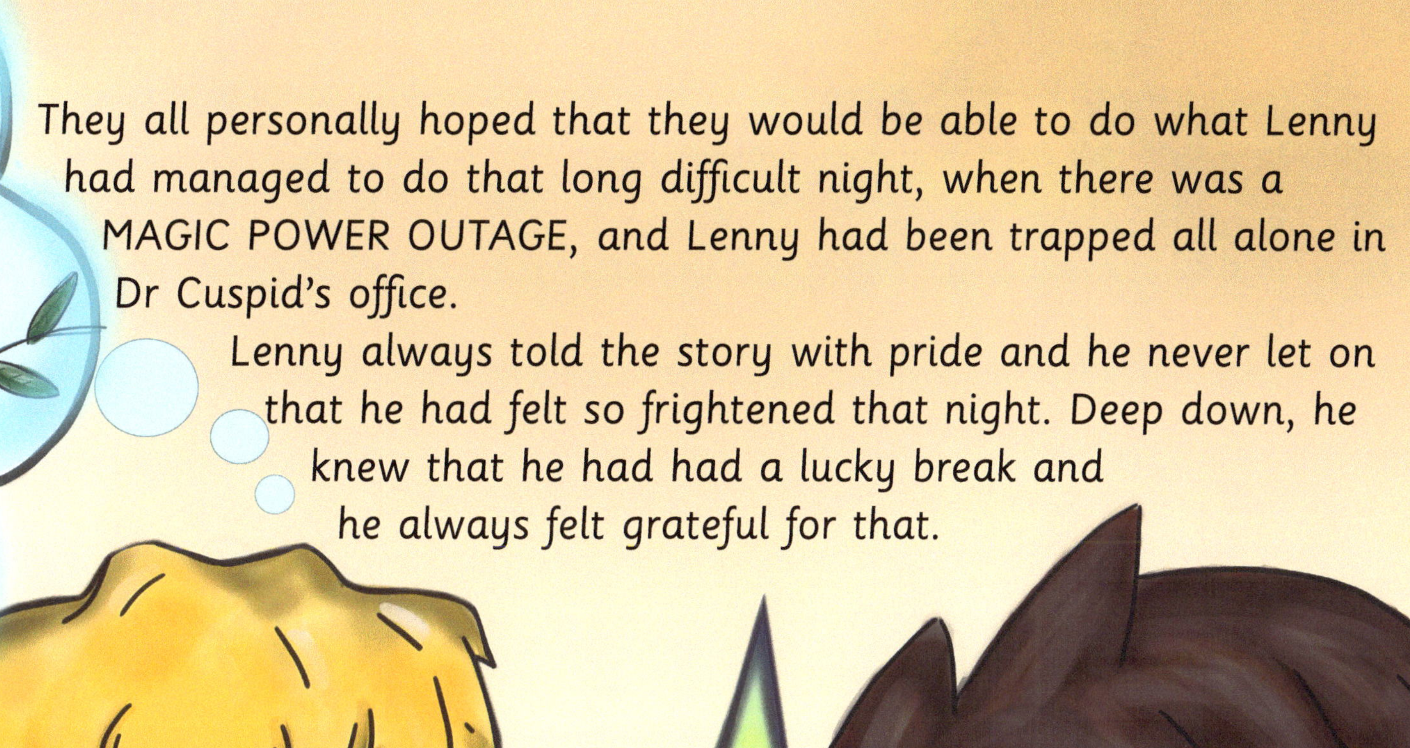

That day the Tooth Technicians had received word that Dr Cuspid had 4 Wisdom Teeth booked to be taken out late that afternoon. The patient, a young girl, would be there for quite a while till Dr Cuspid had extracted not 1 not 2 not 3 but 4 BIG WISDOM TEETH!

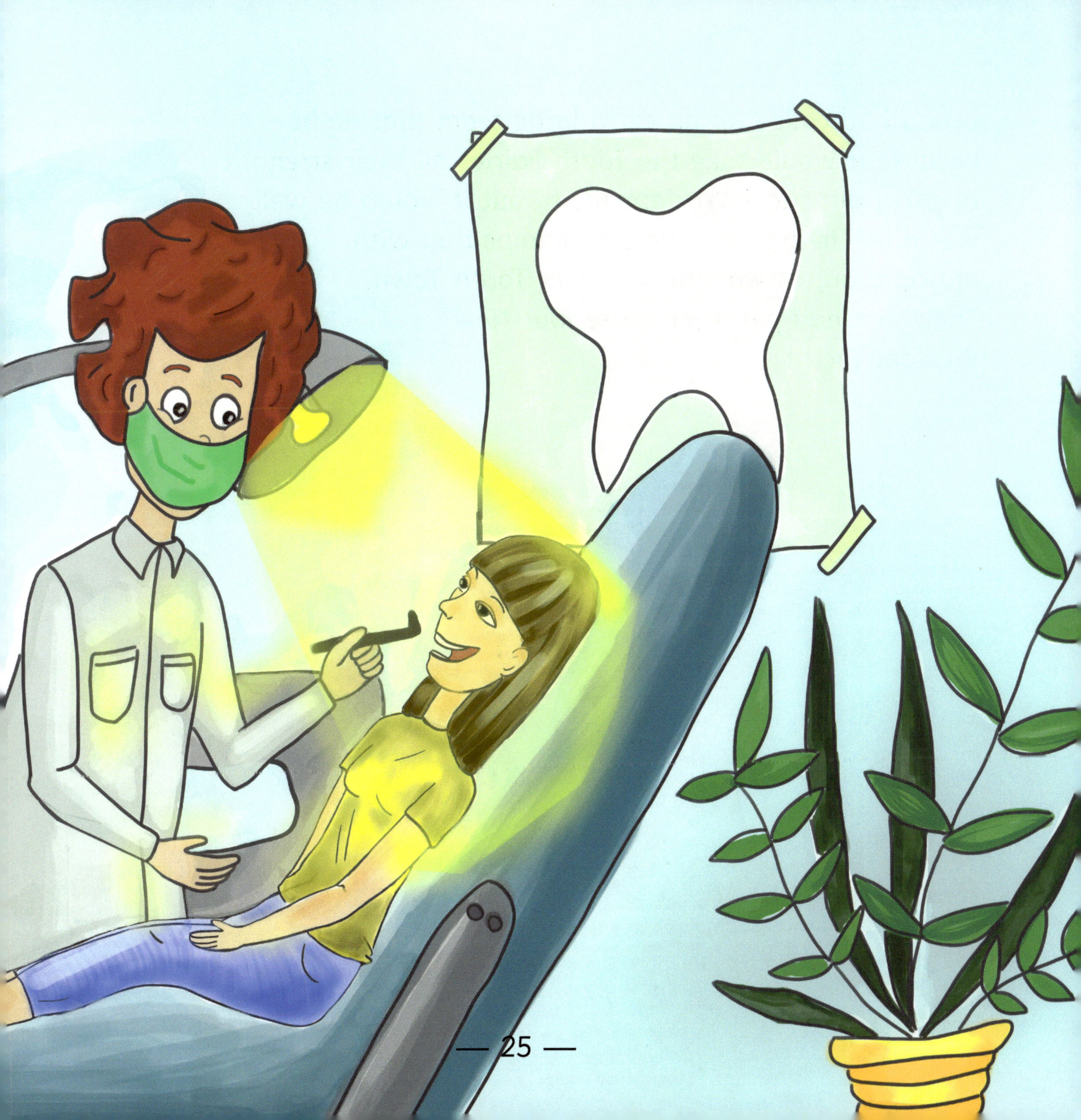

Lenny had called up an extra large team that night because it would take the Tooth Fairies all their strength to carry out those Wisdom Teeth, but it would be well worth it. The whole team was pumped up with anticipation, as was the whole of Tooth Town. They sure had plans for those four New Wisdom Teeth!

They were to be used for the new Tooth Spa for Tired Tooth
Team Members where wings were mended and tired Fairies
were given an energy boost of
Tooth Town smoothies
throughout the day.

The extra large Tooth Taxi pulled up
outside the entrance of Dr Cuspid's office.
Lenny jumped out, Tooth Tote in hand and instructed
the team to follow in a moment after he checked that
everyone had left the office.

TT

You see, Tooth Fairies are ever so small and really can't be seen or heard by humans. There is often the danger of getting SQUISHED. Tooth Teams have on occasion, returned home to Tooth Town saddened with the loss of a Tooth Team Member who had been TRODDEN on by a Mom or Dad or even worse, pounced on by a cat, because animals *CAN* see Tooth Fairies.

Lenny was cautious and experienced and his Tooth Team trusted him implicitly. However, no sooner had Lenny sailed in through the walls when the TROUBLE TONE began to emit a BEEP-BEEP-BEEP in the Tooth Taxi. The POWER was out. Lenny was trapped inside and couldn't get out!

The Tooth Fairies were silent.
They knew that they only had
a short amount of time in the
human world before they would
begin to get that feeling of being so very TIRED
and then they wouldn't have the strength to return home.

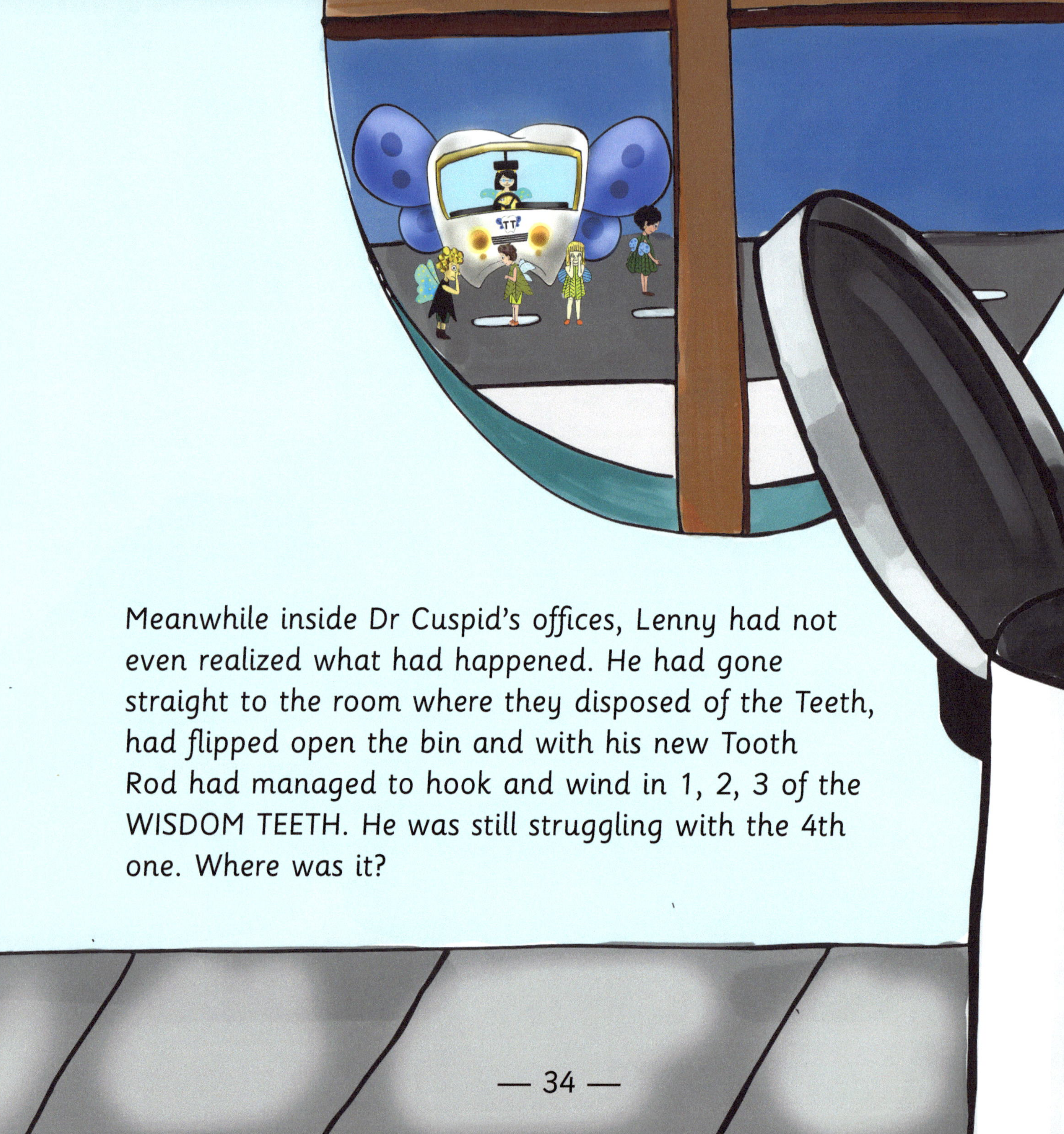

Meanwhile inside Dr Cuspid's offices, Lenny had not even realized what had happened. He had gone straight to the room where they disposed of the Teeth, had flipped open the bin and with his new Tooth Rod had managed to hook and wind in 1, 2, 3 of the WISDOM TEETH. He was still struggling with the 4th one. Where was it?

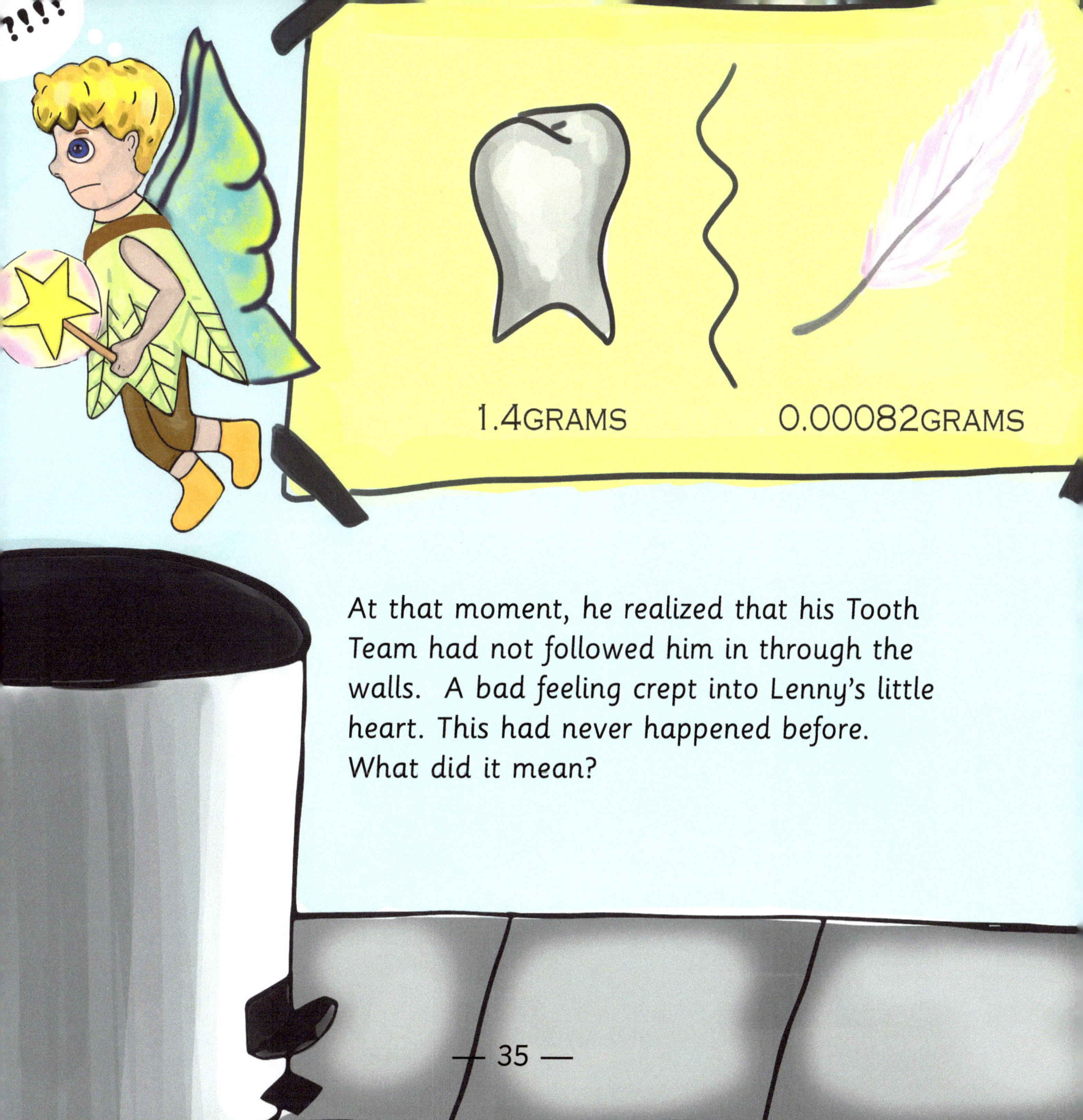

At that moment, he realized that his Tooth Team had not followed him in through the walls. A bad feeling crept into Lenny's little heart. This had never happened before. What did it mean?

He scurried out the door and flew straight at the walls and PHOOOOM...he almost knocked himself out! There was no way through the walls. He was STUCK and no one could help him. A POWER OUTAGE! Lenny shivered and thought sadly "This is it. I will never see TOOTH TOWN again...what an end!"

1.4GRAMS
0.000

T T

Up in Tooth Town there was an uproar at the Tooth Terminal. Everyone had heard the alarm and knew that there was a stranded Tooth Team! All the fairies gathered around. Their voices were high-pitched and nervous.

Lenny suddenly sat up and muttered "Find a way! I have to find a way." He began to rush around, in and out of offices he had never explored on his visits to Dr Cuspid. Suddenly, he heard the sound of wheels and the tap-tap-tap of shoes coming closer and closer. Lenny remembered that the cleaning company also had entry into Dr Cuspid's office after hours.

Maybe, just maybe, this was a way out but what about the WISDOM TEETH? Lenny was not strong enough to do this alone but he HAD to! What about the Tooth Spa for Tired Tooth Team Members?

Lenny made up his mind. He
quickly pushed the 4 BIG WISDOM
TEETH into a pile, grabbed
a paper towel, opened it up
diagonally and tightly rolled up
the teeth and shoved it into the
Tooth Tote

Puffing and panting, Lenny then rolled his precious package towards the cleaning cart, clutching it close to him. Lenny fluttered his wings and with a huge leap and some desperate flapping of his wings, which nearly TOPPLED him, he made it to the top of the cart.

The cart began to move at great speed, and Lenny held on, just barely, still clutching the TEETH. The doors were opened and before you could say TINY TEETH Lenny found himself outside. He rolled off the cart staggering under the weight of the FOUR Big Wisdom Teeth. He spotted the Tooth Taxi but was too tired to call out. He just collapsed and squeaked "Tooth T-e-a-m"

TT
TT

Meanwhile the Tooth Team
had spread out and Tiny Tony, who was indeed tiny,
shrieked as he spotted Lenny lying on the ground.
He gave a shrill whistle and soon the entire Tooth
Team surrounded Lenny and pushed and shoved and
PUUUUULLED him and the Wisdom Teeth towards the
Tooth Taxi.

By now Lenny had woken up and saw that he was aboard! At least the team was safe in the Tooth Taxi, although it seemed they were still STRANDED. Suddenly they realized that the beep-beep-beep had stopped. The power was ON! With happy squeals they took off back to Tooth Town.

Terminal

Lenny smiled as he remembered the huge welcome they received that night. Warmth flooded through him and his wings fluttered. He felt like he was floating through the air on the waves of the celebration all around him.
Lenny smiled to himself as he stood proudly looking out at the beginnings of the new Tooth Spa for Tired Tooth Team Members, knowing that he had contributed the very first FOUR Big Wisdom Teeth!

Who knew what big adventures still awaited him?

About the author

Oriane is an elementary school teacher in Toronto, Canada. This is her first children's book. *Lenny and the Tooth Town Team* was written years ago but waited to be illustrated and printed for many years. It had a solid place on her bucket list until she decided it was time to go ahead. She hopes it will be the first of many children's books that will be read and reread by young readers.

Learn more at orianefalkenstein.com
To learn more about the Lenny series and for some great reader activities please go to lennyandthetoothteam.com

www.ingramcontent.com/pod-product-compliance
Lightning Source LLC
Chambersburg PA
CBHW042116030726
47599CB00002B/244